The Little Llama Meets a Unicorn

The Little Llama's Adventures, Book 1

Isla Wynter

This book belongs to

_____

Once upon a time, Lila the little llama decided she wanted to meet a unicorn.

She'd heard a lot about unicorns, but had never seen one.

Have you ever seen a unicorn?

has a horn

likes rainbows

covered in glitter

looks like a horse

First, she made a list of what she knew about unicorns. It wasn't very much.

The most important thing she knew that unicorns were always seen near rainbows.

If Lila wanted to find a unicorn, she just needed to look for a rainbow!

Lila travelled to the desert and looked around. She didn't find a rainbow, only lots and lots of sand and cacti.

She realised that rainbows only happen when there's rain.

The desert was the wrong place to look for a rainbow!

In the forest, Lila met a very sleepy sloth.

"Have you seen a rainbow?" she asked.

The sloth yawned and shook his head, then went back to sleep.

"Sorry for waking you," Lila whispered and tiptoed away.

After a long journey, Lila came to the sea. And because she was a very lucky llama, it started to rain just when she arrived!

She remembered what her auntie had told her once: You need to look away from the sun to see a rainbow.

But where was the sun?

A whoooooosh of wind blew one of the clouds away and behind it, the sun peeked out.

Lila was very happy. She turned away from the sun and searched for a rainbow.

Can you see one?

Lila looked left and right and suddenly, she could see a unicorn running towards her.

"Hello!" she shouted.

The unicorn whinnied and presented its glittering horn.

"You're not like a horse," Lila said.

She was confused. This unicorn didn't look like a horse at all.

It looked like a llama!

"I'm a llamacorn," the strange creature replied. "I was a llama and decided to be like a unicorn, so I became a llamacorn."

Lila nodded. That made sense.

Of course a llama wouldn't become a unicorn. It would become a llamacorn.

"Can I become a llamacorn too?" she asked.

The llamacorn nodded.
"If you really want to. You have to believe in magic and you have to make people happy. Can you do that?"

Lila smiled.

"How do I become a llamacorn?" Lila asked.

"You need to say the magic words," her new friend replied.

Lila smiled. That was easy.

She took a deep breath and said…

I BELIEVE IN UNICORNS

When Lila said the magic words, the ground shook and a rainbow formed above them and glitter fell from the sky.

Suddenly, she felt something heavy on her forehead.

"You have a horn," the llamacorn told her with a smile.

The two llamacorns quickly became friends and went on many adventures.

They told the magic words to other animals who also wanted to become unicorns.

And now, you also know the magic words…

Are you ready to become a unicorn?

Other books by Isla

The Little Llama Meets a Unicorn
The Little Llama Gets a Cat
The Little Llama Dreams of Space
The Little Llama Learns About Christmas

Once Upon a Unicorn

Lucy the Mermaid and the Easter Egg Hunt

The Day Grandpa Bunny Forgot Ben's Name

The Little Ghost Who Didn't Want to be Scary

About Isla Wynter

Isla Wynter lives in Scotland with two cuddly bunnies, a lonely pot plant and a horde of imaginary friends.
She believes in unicorns and plans to one day convince the world of that fact.
Until then, she continues to write stories for children and young adults.

Follow her on Facebook and Instagram, or subscribe to her newsletter: islawynter.com.

Printed in Poland
by Amazon Fulfillment
Poland Sp. z o.o., Wrocław